Best Friends Forever

by Owen Hart Illustrated by Judi Abbot

tiger tales

Some friends are funny . . .

. . . some friends are **wise**.

And some make you smile
with a happy surprise!

Some friends are playful—
some friends are brave.

And some melt your heart
with a warm little wave.

Some friends are **kind**
and know just what to say,

Bringing the sunshine
to brighten your day.

Friends can be found
everywhere you might go,

But there's one friend more special
than any I know...

Who hears all my secrets,
who shares in my fun,
Who thinks up adventures
to have in the sun.

There's simply no end
to the things we can do.
My best friend forever
will always be . . .

...you!

tiger tales
5 River Road, Suite 128, Wilton, CT 06897
Published in the United States 2018
Originally published in Great Britain 2018
by Little Tiger Press
Text by Owen Hart
Text copyright © 2018 Little Tiger Press
Illustrations copyright © 2018 Judi Abbot
ISBN-13: 978-1-68010-085-3
ISBN-10: 1-68010-085-8
Printed in China
LTP/1400/1973/0917
All rights reserved
10 9 8 7 6 5 4 3 2 1

For more insight and activities, visit us at www.tigertalesbooks.com